The River of No Return

A Lucky Penny Rafting Adventure

ISBN (paperback) 978-1-941420-47-8

Cover & Interior Design: Tru Publishing
www.trupublishing.com

Printed in the United States

The River of No Return

A Lucky Penny Rafting Adventure

Craig Vroom

Illustrated by
Jenn Chic

Tru Publishing
Boise, USA

Contents

Chapter 1—The Request..................................1

Chapter 2—The Packing 5

Chapter 3—The Planning 9

Chapter 4—The Launch 15

Chapter 5—The Background..............................19

Chapter 6—The Campfire 23

Chapter 7—The Jump....................................27

Chapter 8—The History.................................31

Chapter 9—The Contest 33

Chapter 10—The Skit...................................37

Chapter 11—The Falls..................................39

Chapter 12—The Ledge..................................45

Chapter 13—The Discovery 49

Chapter 14—The Soak...................................53

Chapter 15—The Haystack...............................57

Chapter 16—The Ride...................................61

Chapter 17—The Dream 65

Contents

Chapter 18—The Interlopers.................................69

Chapter 19—The Cave..73

Chapter 20—The Kayaking 77

Chapter 21—The Rescue 81

Chapter 22—The Stories..85

Chapter 23—The Favorite Part............................89

Chapter 24—The Big Water 91

Chapter 25—The Rocks..93

Chapter 26—The Finish..95

Chapter 27—The Lucky Penny 99

Chapter 28—The Postscript 103

Glossary of River Terms 105

The River Campfire Song 106

Acknowledgments...107

Dedication

To the good men and women of AWeSOMe and Team River Runner. You inspire us all.

Chapter 1

The Request

"**W**ell, Olivia. This is going to be quite the adventure!" exclaimed Jenny as the two of them ate breakfast. "We will be rafting down the River of No Return with the president of the United States!"

The week before, the Lucky Penny Detectives had received a call from the White House requesting that they join the president and her daughter on a rafting vacation! A Secret Service agent had called and had asked them if they were available to help escort President Langford and her daughter Sara on their journey down the Middle Fork of the Salmon River, a wild river in the middle of Idaho.

"We want you to blend in, keep Sara company, and provide an added measure of safety and security for the

president's daughter," said Agent Dan Reppard enthusiastically. "You've been recommended to us by the Forest Service for your work in helping solve the Yellowstone Yeti mystery a few years ago. We also know that you have experience in rafting the Middle Fork and that you both have CPR and first aid certification.

We've already run background checks on you, and you both passed with flying colors. Do you accept the task?"

It would be their most challenging assignment to date. Olivia had thought for a second and then, lifting her eyebrows, had looked at Jenny while nodding her head yes. Jenny had broken into a wide grin. They could read each other like a book!

"Yes!" Olivia had exclaimed back into the phone, "a thousand times, yes!"

On the other end of the phone, Agent Reppard was grinning too. "OK, here's what we need you to do. . ."

Chapter 2

The Packing

"The key is to pack efficiently for this trip," said a thoughtful Olivia. "We'll be on the river for six days and five nights and there isn't a lot of room on those rafts for non-essential stuff." Olivia turned to Jenny. "Here's a list I made up yesterday. Take a look at it and see if I left anything off."

Jenny looked the list over. "Pajamas. It gets pretty cold at night. And what about floppy hats to avoid sunburn? And those thingies that keep your glasses from falling off into the river. I noticed that you didn't forget our Lucky Penny. We had a near disaster when we forgot it for that Kenya safari case!"

"Yep. We don't go anywhere without the Lucky Penny. OK, good. I guess that's everything. And, because there is no Wi-Fi", Olivia continued, "we'll bring three walkie-talkies—two for us and one for the president's daughter. There's no cell coverage where we are going! Oh, and even though our outfitters and guides will provide our food during the journey, let's put in a few healthy snacks as well."

"I wonder what she's like," said Jenny pensively.

"Who?"

"Sara!"

"Well, we know she likes books and school, and she *did* ask to go on this trip, so she can't be all bad."

"I hope she's not a crab apple!" Jenny blurted out. That was a term Jenny used for someone who was always negative, who always saw the glass as half-empty. "If she's a crab apple, it's going to be a long trip!"

"I'm sure she'll be fine as soon as we get on the river. Speaking of the river, we've got to make sure we're prepared for anything and everything."

"Yeah, the River of No Return is something everyone should take very seriously," exclaimed Jenny. "It probably gets its name from people who went off unprepared for the hazards of a wilderness river journey. Nature can be cruel at times, especially on an unpredictable river! That's why we will be super-prepared for this adventure!"

"Yep," Olivia commented. "I was looking at the average river heights for this time of year. The water is running pretty high for late June. It's going to take good maps and a lot of confidence to navigate the rumbling waters of Cramer Creek!"

"And the big water of Rubber Rapids!" interjected Jenny. "And don't forget Veil Cave Rapids. That can really leap out and bite you if you're not careful!"

"Well, we're scheduled to meet with Marvin and his crew on Thursday," Olivia said. "They're going to go over all the rapids and explain how we should run them. Let's take good notes and then memorize them!"

Chapter 3

The Planning

John Gisler began the descent of his Cessna 206, avoiding the treetops and the canyon walls, and aimed his aircraft toward the Thomas Creek runway. Gisler leveled the plane's wings, made smooth contact with the ground, and brought the aircraft to a stop by a small building. Olivia and Jenny breathed a sigh of relief and worked their way out of their seats, glad to be back on land.

"Notch up another safe and successful flight into the wilderness!" Olivia exclaimed.

"Yeah, a successful flight, in my mind, is when you don't need the barf bag!" joked Jenny.

They retrieved their gear and crossed the footbridge to the other side of the river. This place was miles from nowhere. This was the spot where they would launch their rafts and begin their sixty-four-mile journey. But first they would have to prepare for the arrival of the president and her entourage.

A host of US Forest Service and security personnel had been landing in small planes from Salmon and Boise throughout the morning. After months of preparation, they felt confident that they had done everything humanly possible to ensure the president would have a safe and memorable journey down the river. President Adele Langford, her daughter Sara, and three Secret Service personnel would be the last to arrive.

President Langford had been looking forward to the Salmon River adventure ever since Sara had asked if they could spend this year's vacation running the river. But she'd made one thing very clear to the Secret Service agents and staff before the detailed planning had begun: "I want this to be a wilderness adventure, not another photo opportunity for the media. Sara and I want to see eagles and bighorn sheep, not a bunch of security guards and cameras! Keep your distance and let us enjoy nature!"

Everyone involved had taken her wishes to heart but, at the same time, they still had a job to do: protect the president and her family. Two Secret Service agents, a Forest Service guide, and a rescue swimmer would be in the large sweep boat with the president. The Deibert

Brothers, a river guide service with over twenty years of experience, would have their two best men taking turns driving the sweep boat. Olivia, Jenny, and a young Secret Service agent named Alex would be in one of the smaller rafts with Sara. Two other rafts would carry rescue swimmers and provisions. Four kayakers, two fore and two aft, would make up the remainder of the president's detail. Everyone else involved, from communications personnel to the president's personal physician, would be on other boats either around the next bend or behind them, safely out of sight.

"Jenny! There's the Marine One helicopter!" Olivia shouted in anticipation. "And there's the president!"

President Langford was the first to step out. The president had her brown hair tied in a ponytail and covered by a Washington Nationals baseball cap. She was wearing jeans, boots, and a hoodie. Olivia thought that the president looked normal, instead of, well, presidential. The president gave everyone a big smile and waved to the security detail and the other adventurers. Olivia waved back, thinking that the president had looked right at her.

Next off the helicopter was Sara. She immediately looked around as if she wanted to take in all of the Idaho wilderness at once. She had red hair and freckles and was a little taller than Jenny remembered from the photos. She exclaimed, "Wow, it's even more beautiful than the pictures!"

"I guess she's not a crab apple," Jenny whispered to Olivia. They both smiled, knowing the trip was looking up already.

Forest Ranger Paul Sheldon was waiting for everyone at Little Creek Guard Station, ready to give them the talk that was necessary for all those rafting the Middle Fork. He had given this spiel hundreds of times over his twenty-plus years as a ranger. A few movie and TV celebrities had come his way before, but this was the first time he had ever addressed anyone as important as a president. He adjusted his wide-brimmed hat as the president's group finished crossing the footbridge.

"Welcome, Madame President, to a true wilderness experience! You and your party are going to have a great time! You're starting your adventure at mile thirty-six of the Middle Fork of the Salmon and you will be completing your journey at Cache Bar near mile 100. The Middle Fork is nature at its finest! You'll be surrounded by walls of granite, placid pools of green water, and dazzling white rapids! You're entering the territory of wild animals. You might see some eagles, a great horned owl, and maybe some bighorn sheep. Every now and then, some rafters see a black bear or two. And fishing is great—especially trout. Take time to see the pictographs left behind by native tribes."

Sara looked at her mom with a big grin on her face. "This is really cool," she whispered.

Ranger Sheldon continued. "You won't find any

cigarette butts, soda cans, or candy wrappers. You won't even see any dental floss. I want all of you to understand that your experience here will be very special . . . but it is up to all of you to leave everything—the river, the shoreline, the campsites, the trees, everything—in the same condition you found them in for those that follow you."

Everyone seemed very thoughtful as they listened to Ranger Sheldon.

"And for your safety, when you're off the river, stay on the trails. Listen to your river guides! Any questions? OK. Enjoy your float. And stay safe!"

June 23rd (day)

Dear Diary,

Yesterday we flew in Air Force One to Boise, Idaho to begin our vacation. This morning, Marine One took us deep into the Frank Church Wilderness. Mom promised me this trip over six months ago—and now we are all ready to float the river! After we landed, we were introduced to the crew. I met my guides, Olivia and Jenny. They are the Lucky Penny Detectives who will stay with me during our trip. They seem nice. I am so excited!

Sara

Chapter 4

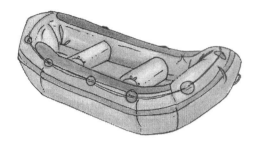

The Launch

The boats were all ready. Provisions were stowed. Marvin and his crew gave a safety brief about how to get in and out of kayaks and what to do if someone went into the water. "You'll have your personal flotation devices, or PDFs, on at all times when on the river," instructed Marvin. "If you go in, get your feet pointing downstream and watch for rocks until we can get to you. And show us you're OK by patting your head with your hand."

Everyone began to feel a sense of anticipation. The lead kayakers were ready. The president and her agents got into the sweep boat. Marvin and his crew eased it into the water.

"And away we go!" shouted Olivia as she took the

first turn on the oars. Pulling away from the shore, Olivia guided the rubber raft into the gently flowing current. As kayakers and rafters began paddling, a bald eagle cruised over the river about 100 feet above them. It was a beauty! Sunlight glinted off of its pure white head. Our national bird nodded its head from side to side as it searched for its next meal. One of the transportation crew members, a Native American named Jim who was staying behind to move vehicles and trailers, enthusiastically exclaimed to all, "This is a wonderful sign! It means that all of you will have a safe and successful journey!"

A sense of peace fell over the party as they listened to the soft murmuring of the river. No one spoke. The canyon walls reached over a thousand feet above them, standing watch like silent sentinels. For those who were rafting for the first time, it was a true adventure into the unknown. For those with river experience, the beginning of a trip was always exciting. But on this trip, they all felt an exaggerated sense of responsibility.

The seasoned guides knew that anything could happen on the river. They also knew that every river trip was a little different from the last. Water flow on the river changed with the seasons and with the amount of snowpack that had accumulated over the winter. This year, the water was flowing higher than normal. Rapids that seemed easy to traverse one year could be filled with dangers the next. Rock exposures changed and a new "hole" could pop up and spin you around when you least expected it. The guides all hoped that they would have a fun-filled, accident-free trip and arrive safely to Cache Bar.

The majesty of this river wilderness area was hard to describe. Sara had never seen such beauty. The sheer granite canyon walls made her feel that she was inside a huge cathedral. And then, when she began to get used to that, the canyon would open up to one of the many tributaries in the river and she would stare in wonder at the rugged and snow-capped Salmon River Mountains. At ten thousand feet tall, they were some of the highest in Idaho. This was going to be an amazing experience.

The silence was temporarily broken by a helicopter passing directly overhead. It was carrying one of the president's security teams. It was yet another reminder that this was no ordinary trip.

Sara looked up to watch the helicopter go around

the next bend. After a brief pause, she said, "Is that still the helicopter making that rumble?"

Just then, Jenny hollered, "That's Jackass Rapids ahead! Remember that large boulder and hole!"

Jackass was listed in the guidebooks as a section of class III rapids—it was usually easy to navigate but still made a rafter sit up and take notice. With the river at over 5.5 feet deep at the Middle Fork Lodge, even the easy ones could sometimes throw challenges at an experienced guide. The rumble grew louder and, a few minutes later, became a roar.

"Stay right to avoid that boulder!" yelled Marvin, leading the way.

Olivia pulled hard on her left oar, bringing the nose of the boat around. "Hold on tight, Sara!"

Down into the churning water they went, the current trying to turn the boat sideways. Up came the nose of the boat—then abruptly down it went as they went over a ledge, spraying them all with the chilly river water. A few jerks left and right and, as quickly as it started, it was over. Once again, they were riding a placid stream.

"That was fun! Let's do that again!" yelled Sara.

"Oh, we'll do it again all right . . . and again, and again!" exclaimed Olivia with a big smile. "Heck, we're just getting started!"

Chapter 5

The Background

S ara was beginning to warm up to the girls. She liked their easy-going personalities, which made her feel comfortable.

"So, Sara—we hear you like to read books. Is there any particular kind of book you like to read? Like . . . adventure stories or mysteries?" asked Jenny.

"All kinds, really. I like mysteries. And I like books with lots of action like *Harry Potter*. But I also like historical fiction and the classics, like *Silas Marner* and *A Tale of Two Cities*. I read a lot. Sometimes two books a week. Depends on how much homework I have."

"Wow. That's a lot of reading. I might read a book a month, if I'm lucky! What about sports? Do you play any sports?" asked Jenny.

"I like playing chess. Does that qualify as a sport? And I like soccer—but I'm not very good at it. Once I had a shot on a goal from five yards and totally wiffed the ball! Coach said I should take up curling!"

"Hey, we all have our moments!" laughed Olivia.

"I *like* curling," muttered Jenny.

Olivia and Jenny then regaled Sara with stories about playing on the Lucky Pennies softball team. "Do you remember, Olivia, when we stole the other team's signs? I think we were playing the Charlotte Stingrays. We knew what the pitcher was going to throw before she threw it! Then there was the time . . ."

Sara kind of tuned them out for a few minutes and let the sounds of the river ease her mind. No DC traffic, no agents hovering . . . Alex was sitting next to her but he seemed to be enjoying the wilderness as much as she was.

". . . but that's a far cry from working the river," Jenny continued. "We've worked super-hard to become guides on the Middle Fork. And it's been worth it!"

Sara really admired them for that and for how they'd showed no fear in the way they had maneuvered their boat through the rapids. She wished she had been brought up in the West, learning outdoor skills like fire-building, tracking, and how to identify edible plants. But Sara's background was big cities and prep schools.

Sara thought back to the time when her mother had been the dean of students at Harvard Business School.

They had lived an idyllic life back then. It seemed like longer than five years ago. Her dad had still been still alive, and had been a big part of her life. They'd done almost everything together. When the skiing accident took him away from them, Sara withdrew into books and schoolwork. She really needed a friend, but it was difficult to keep a relationship going when she didn't get out much and, when she did, she had Secret Service agents watching her every move.

Sara knew she had needed a break from the pressures of school and the rat race of DC. About six months ago, she had decided to do her school research paper on the River of No Return. She'd dug deep into the history of the Middle Fork and the Main Salmon. She'd read the passed-down stories about the hardships faced by early Idaho miners and pioneers, like Polly Bemis, the Chinese woman who'd befriended the settlers and provided them with food while on the river. Brought to the United States from China as a slave, Polly had overcome racial prejudice and had become one of Idaho's greatest pioneers. Her cabin, known as the Polly Bemis house, was eventually placed on the National Register of Historic Places. And then there was Fritz (Stovepipe) Music, who'd walked around with metal stovepipes strapped to his legs in case the rattlesnakes decided to strike. These were some real characters! Reading about this wilderness took her back to what seemed like 100 years ago, back to a time when everyone had to live off the land; a far cry from the hectic, suburban lives lived by those in the nation's capital. It was then that she had asked—no, *begged*—her mother for a vacation down the river.

The screech of an osprey brought Sara back to reality from her daydreaming just in time to see the party edging over to the shore at Pine Flat Camp for lunch.

"OK, everybody. This will be our first lunch stop!" exclaimed Marvin. "And bring your appetites! We have sandwiches, fruit, and cookies for everyone."

Chapter 6

The Campfire

*T*hat evening, they pulled into White Creek Camp after an afternoon of casual floating. Everyone went to work pitching their tents while the crew set up the "kitchen" for the evening meal.

Rusty, the head cook, rang the dinner bell and announced to all, "Dinner tonight is steak, baked potatoes, and green beans. And, for dessert, apple pie! A meal fit for a king . . . err, a president!"

Everyone got a chuckle out of that as they queued up for dinner.

After dinner, two of the rescue swimmers, Andrew Vogt and Aaron Olsen, collected driftwood and began building a campfire. Everyone grabbed a beach chair and settled in around the fire for what many call one of the most wonderful traditions of river rafting: a campfire and some music. Aaron came back from his tent with his guitar.

"Here's a song I wrote after my first trip down the Middle Fork. It's called 'The River Campfire,' and it goes like this:

"The river campfire wakens—reaching toward the sky.
Listen to it crackle. Listen to it sigh.
It starts to light the campground—sand and grass and tree.
Lighting up our faces. Light for you and me.

"The river campfire's burning—such a pretty sight.
Telling us its stories. Putting off the night.
Hear the river riffle, softly by us flowing.
Listen to our laughter. Friendships ever growing.

"The river campfire's blazing—throwing out its darts.
Feel it light our bodies. Feel it warm our hearts.
Framing storytellers under granite halls.
Of Devil's Molar Rapids. Running Tappan Falls.

"The river campfire's glowing—the fire's at an end.
Warming every stranger. Touching every friend.
It's time for soft reflection. Laying down to rest.
We're thankful for the river.
We are truly blessed."

"The river separates us all.
For all the skilled—excites us.
For all the rookies—short, the tall,
The river often bites us.
But the campfire, oh the campfire
The campfire. . . . . .unites us.

With that, everyone started heading for bed, reflecting on this beautiful experience they had all been sharing.

June 23rd (night)

Dear Diary,

This evening was like a dream! After dinner, one of the swimmers pulled out his guitar and we sang songs around the campfire. I haven't seen Mom so relaxed in a long time. We both smiled at each other, knowing that this vacation was exactly what we both needed. And Aaron—I think it was Aaron (I get Andrew and Aaron mixed up)—sang a really cool song about the campfire. Everybody sang along and had a blast!

Later....as I was walking toward our tent to turn in for the night, I looked up at the Idaho sky. OMG! It looked like there were about a million stars up there! I thought.....so this is what the sky looked like before street lights and big cities! Amazing!

Sara

Chapter 7

The Jump

*D*awn broke the next morning on one of those beautiful late June days in Idaho: crystal clear yet cool enough to still need a jacket. After all, they were at an elevation of over five thousand feet. Sara couldn't see the sun yet—it was blocked by the canyon walls—but she could feel its presence. She had slept like a log last night. She had crawled into her sleeping bag, adjusted her pillow, and let out a contented sigh. She had listened to the soft flow of the river, thinking how lucky she was to be on this adventure. That's the last thing she remembered.

Now it was daylight and the river was still running smooth and slow. *It ran all night long while we were asleep*, Sara thought. *Runs all day too. Just keeps running.*

How many thousands of years has water been flowing by this spot?

Marvin and his crew were already working on breakfast. This morning they were cooking pancakes and bacon. Everything smelled so good. Sara searched out her mom. There she was—having coffee and talking with Olivia — something about a bridge.

"We've done it loads of times and the guides will back me up," said Olivia. "Almost everybody tries it—if they're not too afraid of heights."

The president looked into her coffee as if thinking about something else. Finally, after a long pause, she said with a smile, "I'll talk to the guides. If they say it is safe, I'll give her the OK."

"What are you giving the OK to, Mom?" Sara inquired as she approached the group.

"Olivia and Jenny want to jump off the White Creek Pack Bridge and they want you to join them. I told them I wasn't sure you'd even want to but they felt that they should ask me first before asking you."

"How high up is this bridge?"

"Olivia says about thirty feet."

"Wow! That's like three times as high as the high diving board at the Georgetown pool."

"It's a ton of fun!" interjected Jenny, who had just joined them. "It's always just a little bit scary but we've never had any trouble doing it. We're going to hike up there soon if you want to jump."

After talking to Marvin, President Langford reluctantly gave Sara permission. "But I'm sending Alex with you! And we'll have a kayak in the water nearby, just in case!"

"Oh, Mom, you worry too much! Everything will be fine!"

Alex and the three girls joined the rest of the crew that was going to make the leap. They headed up the trail for the pack bridge about a quarter-mile away.

Sara watched intently as each crew member jumped. She wanted to get this right. She realized that she was

next in line. She positioned herself so that her feet were on the railing and so that she could still hang on to one of the crossbars.

"One, two, three, go!" yelled Olivia and Jenny together.

Sara closed her eyes, held her nose, and jumped. The water rushed up to meet her. It felt so cold that it almost took her breath away! But she got her bearings, came to the surface, and patted her head: the OK sign. Everybody cheered!

"Now, that is what the West is all about!" she screamed to the delight of all around.

June 24th (Day)

Dear Diary,

Today was one of the best days of my life! I can't believe that we are out in the wilderness of Idaho, drinking in its splendors. We jumped off a HUGE bridge! Mom was cool about it. I was so scared, I almost wet my pants! But Olivia and Jenny got me through it and I'm super glad they did. I proved to myself that I can fit in with all these Westerners.

I even held my own when someone started a water fight. We had a water gun made for shooting a big stream at someone, so I aimed it at one of our kayakers. Of course, he returned fire at us using his paddle. When that happened, it was a full-bore battle. What fun! I can't wait until tomorrow!

Sara

Chapter 8

The History

*A*fter spending an hour or so at the bridge, the party pulled into Big Loon Camp for lunch.

"Mom, it says here in the book I've been reading, that this place has some interesting history. Do you want me to read it to you?"

"Sure. Go for it!"

"This was the site of a gold discovery in May of 1869 at Loon Creek, a Middle Fork tributary. By August, there were over five hundred miners working the river! After a few years, only the Chinese miners stayed on to prospect. In February of 1879, five of the Chinese miners were killed. Locals accused—without proof— a local Shoshone tribe, the Tukudeka, also known as the Sheepeaters, claiming they had murdered the Chinese.

As a result, the US military was ordered in to track them down and drive them out of the area. When about fifteen Tukudeka warriors attacked the troops guarding a pack train, the battle was on. This conflict became known as the Sheepeater Wars. It was the last Indian war fought in the Northwest."

"Interesting. I didn't know anything about that. Why did they call them Sheepeaters? Does it say?"

Sara scanned the chapter. "It says they got their name because they were really good at hunting Rocky Mountain sheep. They were nomadic—they moved around a lot, following the wild game. Central Idaho was probably their primary winter home. It says here that the US First Calvary troops had a hard time tracking them down because the wilderness was so inhospitable. Outnumbered and with colder weather approaching, one of the Indian chiefs turned himself in and negotiated a surrender with the soldiers. Fifty-one men, women, and children were taken prisoner. They admitted to attacking the pack train but denied killing the Chinese prospectors."

"Sara, remind me when we get home to look into that. Sounds like they may have been innocent. I want to see if the Tukudeka were ever absolved of those crimes they were accused of."

Chapter 9

The Contest

*A*fter lunch, Marvin announced that there would be a fishing contest between boats.

"Now, the object is to catch as many cutthroat trout as possible in forty-five minutes. They have to measure over twelve inches long. Each boat will have two poles and a twelve-inch stick to use to make sure the fish are worth counting. We have fishing licenses for each of you; however, there are some rules. All fish must be returned to the river. Measure them as best you can while they are still in the water; then release them. Each of you will have a pole with a barbless hook. Any questions?"

Olivia spoke up. "What is the prize for winning?

"How could I forget that?" Marvin said with a gleam

in his eye. "The people in the boat with the most fish don't have to pitch their tents tonight. Others will do that for them. Who, you might ask? The *losers*, of course! The people in the boat with the fewest fish must put up the winners' tents. Plus, the losers have to bow down, show the winners the proper respect, and put on a skit for them at the campfire tonight! Any other questions? Good. Let's get fishing!"

"OK, Sara," instructed Olivia. "You and Alex can go first. Try to cast your line downstream. Jenny will help you with casting, and I'll man the oars. Make sure you cast diagonally, so that we don't snag each other! And, take turns casting. Practice a few times before Marvin blows the horn to start."

Sara was just beginning to get the hang of it when the horn pierced the air. *Honnnnnnnk!* Sara cast her line into the river. It took about ten casts before she hooked her first cutthroat. And, it was a beauty! Olivia measured it at about fourteen inches. Sara unhooked the fish and released it back into the water. "There it goes!" she exclaimed. Alex caught his first fish a few minutes later, and they were off!

After about fifteen minutes, the president yelled "We've got four so far!"

"Well, our raft has caught six!" yelled Sara.

When the horn finally sounded again, everyone took turns reading off the number of fish they had caught.

"The president's boat has eight!"

"Rescue swimmers' boat has eleven!"

"We've only got nine!" said the dejected driver of Boat #4, the one last in line with most of the provisions. "But we only had two people aboard!!"

"Cry me a river!" exclaimed Marvin unsympathetically.

"Our boat has thirteen!" announced Sara.

"We have a winner!" exclaimed Marvin.

A chorus of cheers went up. "Hip-hip-hooray! Hip-hip-hooray!"

"And, we also have a *loser*!" Marvin announced with glee, making an L with his fingers and placing it against his forehead. "See you all tonight at the campfire!"

With a sheepish grin on her face, the president of the United States stared over at the people in Sara's boat and thought to herself, "This is the best decision I've made since I became president."

Chapter 10

The Skit

That night after dinner, Sara's boat team, nicknamed the Paddlers, was asked to return to their tents until they got the signal to come out. The crews from the other boats formed lines facing each other between the tents and the campfire. Everyone held up crossed oars for them to walk under. The president's sweep boat team was waiting for Sara, Olivia, Jenny, and Alex to perform their skit.

"OK. Bring them out! We're ready to give an Oscar-winning performance!" the president announced.

Out came the Paddlers. As they walked the gauntlet, all raised their voices to the reigning fishing champs.

"Hail to the fisher kings!" the other crews shouted. "Long live the Paddlers!"

When the Paddlers reached the campfire, they were met by a bowing president and her crew.

"We salute you, oh great Paddlers. We honor you with a skit worthy of a royal court. Please have a seat on your thrones, and we'll begin!"

The Paddlers sat on tree stumps and logs. Marvin got down on his hands and knees. President Langford stepped up behind him and acted like she was pulling a cord attached to Marvin.

"Rrrrr," Marvin sputtered.

The president pulled the cord once more.

Again, Marvin sputtered "Rrrrr!"

"Doggone it! I just can't get my lawn motor to start. Alex, do you want to give it a try? Maybe a big, strong man like you can get it going!"

"Yes, ma'am. I'll give it a go."

Alex walked up behind Marvin and gave a big, manly pull on the imaginary cord.

Marvin perked right up and bellowed, *"Rrrrrrrrrrrrrrrrrr!"* and started off.

The president then proclaimed, "See? All we needed was a bigger *jerk!*"

Chapter 11

The Falls

"This is Tappan Day!" declared Jenny as she got in line for breakfast at Upper Grouse Camp. "We rafters will really be earning our stripes today!"

"What do you mean by Tappan Day?", asked President Langford.

"This is the day we do the Tappan Rapids," answered Olivia. "The Tappan Rapids are actually a series of six rapids: Tappan Canyon Entrance Rapid—a class II+; followed by Tappan I—a class III. Then comes Tappan Falls—a class III+; followed by Tappan II, a class III-. After that is Tappan III, also called Cove Creek, a class III-. It can be real tricky! Finally, there's Tappan IV, a class II. If we make it through the first five without somebody going into the water, we'll have the lead kayakers stop and take photos."

"Have you ever had problems in the Tappan Rapids?" asked Sara, unaware of its history.

Jenny responded, "We had a raft trip three weeks ago, but the water was significantly higher then. We had some problems with one raft that went too far left and got stuck on Buzzard's Reef. It's not only the challenge of the individual rapids, it's the fact that you can barely catch your breath in between them. The Tappan Rapids will keep you on your toes for over a mile! And everyone, including you, Sara, will have to do their part to get us through this gauntlet safely!"

After breakfast, Marvin gathered the crew and rafters together to go over some of the characteristics of Tappan Rapids. After that meeting, Olivia and Jenny went over each of the rapids, paying particular attention to what Sara and Alex would be expected to do.

Olivia gave them a few more pieces of advice. "And remember, if you fall into the river, get on your back and point your feet downstream! Keep your knees slightly bent. That will allow you to see what's coming, and push off of any rocks with your feet! Keep a good grip on your paddle. There will be the sweeper boat and two kayaks ahead of us that can pick you up. Extend your paddle to them and offer the 'T-grip' end to them so they can pull you in."

The Tappan Rapids were only a mile down the river. Sara was already getting nervous. The river took a big turn to the left. Sara looked up to see a huge, gray, vertical wall of granite. Then there was the familiar dull roar up ahead.

"Tappan Rapids dead ahead!" yelled Marvin.

Jenny was the lead rower this time. She was sitting on the outer rim in the rear of the raft for power and for steering. Olivia had the best view of the river in front. Sara and Alex were between them on the sides.

Olivia sensed a slight drift right. "Stay left, Jenny, and we'll avoid that large boulder downstream!"

Down through the Canyon Entrance Rapids they flew. This was a fun wave ride that didn't require a lot of technical skill. Alex was keeping his cool, but Sara let out a whoop. The river then took a sharp turn back to the right. Tappan I was next.

Olivia then screamed loudly, over the noise of the rushing water, "Stay center and then left of center to avoid the cliff wall!"

"Got it!", yelled Jenny.

They cruised through without incident. Two down, four to go! They entered a calm pool, which didn't stay calm for long. They could now see the whitecaps of Tappan Falls. They waited for the lead boat to go through. The water was drifting the heavy boat left. All of a sudden, the president's boat was caught on the edge of a large "keeper-hole," which began to swirl them around.

"We're Maytagging! Everybody to the high side!" yelled Marvin. Just as quickly as they'd entered, to the relief of all, the "washing machine" spit them back out onto the river.

"Did you see that, Jenny? We have to stay right on this one!" Olivia instructed. "The river's pulling us left! Everybody row *hard* on three! One, two, three!"

Sara began rowing with all her might. She leaned into the stroke and used her body weight to lean back. They just missed the large keeper-hole that would have capsized them! Then, over the falls they went, the raft dipping and bucking them. Sara felt weightless, as if a big hand had reached down and was pulling her up. Back down she came, still trying to keep her oar in the water. They had almost done a 'taco'—where the nose of the raft buckles back toward the middle.

Olivia, still paddling hard, yelled, "Now, keep it straight past the center rock and then work it left!"

Jenny had done a masterful job of guiding the raft past that last hole. They were through the falls! Even Alex got excited about that one. "Yeehaw!" he yelled.

Tappan II was next. This one was also called "Fish and Game Rock" for the large, flat boulder in the center stream.

"We're at high water, so stay right, Jenny!"

They barely squeezed between Fish and Game and another, smaller rock to the right.

"Now, take a hard right to avoid Buzzard's Reef!"

The left rear of their raft just grazed the last rock of Buzzard's Reef, but they managed to stay in the flow that took them through to the end of Tappan II. But Cove Creek was coming up fast.

"We're riding the current on this next one but, near the end, we've got to pull hard right to avoid Old Boulder!"

Into the current of Cove Creek they went, picking up speed quickly, rollicking and rushing past large, jutting rocks, enjoying the rush.

"Bump ahead!"

Everyone pulled their paddles in and leaned toward the center to stabilize their raft as they went over a shallow rock.

"Now, hard right to avoid Old Boulder!"

Everyone rowed as hard and fast as they could, bringing them around to the right and avoiding the last real danger of the Tappan Rapids.

"We did it!" yelled Sara. "We conquered Tappan Falls!"

After that, Tappan IV, a class II, was a mere formality. They began to drift into a large pool. Waiting for them were the sweep boat and the kayakers, who had been taking photographs.

"Good going everybody!" exclaimed Marvin. "We'll be spending the night at Sheep Creek Campground another six miles down the river. But first, let's take advantage of these pools and get in the water for a soak and a swim!"

June 25th (Day)

Dear Diary,

Wow! The Tappan Rapids were awesome! I've never been so scared and excited at the same time. It was a little like riding six different roller coasters in a row. But with the river, there's the added excitement of the unknown. Will we hit that rock? Will we flip if we do? Will we get stuck in a "washing machine?" Olivia and Jenny were unbelievable. They are sooooo good! And we got some great photos. My favorite shows us hurtling through Cove Creek at about a zillion miles per hour!

Sara

Chapter 12

The Ledge

"*L*et's go exploring!" an excited Sara exclaimed. Before Jenny and Olivia could properly beach their raft, Sara had jumped out, removed her PDF, and run up the path toward a cabin near Sheep Creek Camp.

"Wait for us!" yelled Jenny as she grabbed a hiking backpack out of their raft.

Sara had about a hundred-yard lead on the girls. She had decided to check out that old cabin she'd seen from the river. While working her way up toward the cabin, she came across a scenic spot where she could look to the north and see around the next bend of the river. She was surprised to discover a family of bighorn sheep. Wow, they were beauties! And the light around them was awesome. This would make a great photo to post on the internet. She was struggling to get her DSLR camera out of her backpack when a rock supporting her gave way. She was losing her footing! Panicking, she yelled for help as she tried to keep from slipping down the side of the cliff!

Down she went, grabbing at sagebrush to break her fall until, miraculously, her feet came to rest on a ledge. She had only traveled about ten feet!

"Oh my God! Why did I do that?" she chastised herself. She checked out her body and realized she had managed to slide down and land on a narrow ledge without any major injuries. There were a few scrapes on her hands, knees, and elbows, but that was it. Now . . . where was she? The ledge she was on was about forty feet long and maybe six feet wide. There was no way she could work her way back up to the trail. She carefully looked over the ledge and immediately felt dizzy. The dry canyon was over three hundred feet down! She realized there was no escape.

In an ice-cold panic, her first thought was, "Nobody even knows where I am!" But then she thought of Olivia and Jenny—and her walkie-talkie. Luckily, it was strapped to her backpack. She snapped it open and pushed the button. She remembered the call signs they had agreed to use.

"Lucky Pennies, this is Bookworm. Come in! Over."

"Bookworm, this is Jenny. We're following your trail. Are you OK? Over."

"Yes, but I'm standing on a ledge. I lost my footing and fell over the side! I'm OK but I can't get off of here without help! Over."

"Don't worry—we'll be right there with some rope! Over!"

The girls followed Sara's footprints on the trail until they found the drop-off.

"We're here, Sara," yelled Jenny. "Are you still all right?"

"Yeah, I'm OK. I'm really sorry, Jenny. How are you gonna get me out of here?"

Olivia took some climbing rope out of her backpack and tied one end of it to a decent-sized lodgepole pine. Jenny put on the climbing harness, adjusted it to her size, and clipped it to the rope.

"OK, Olivia, lower me down!"

Chapter 13

The Discovery

Olivia slowly lowered Jenny down until her feet gently reached the ledge.

"I am so glad to see you guys!" Sara said happily.

Jenny began to fit Sara into the harness. By now, Alex had joined Olivia and was prepared to help pull Sara and Jenny off the ledge. Just then, something caught Jenny's eye as she faced the cliff wall. It looked like some roughly drawn figures painted in red.

"Hang on a second, Olivia!

Jenny moved a little closer to the rock drawings. These things looked like Indian pictographs. They must have been painted many years ago.

"I've got something I want you to see, Olivia. But first, let's get Sara lifted to safety. Alex can take her back to the boats, and then he can come back to help. But we really need to check this out. This may be a real find!"

After taking care of Sara, Alex came back with help. Jenny had remained on the ledge, taking photographs of the paintings. The first scene, almost perfectly preserved, showed what looked like a ceremony around a campfire. There were five man-like figures holding what looked like tools or weapons. Above the men, there was a larger figure with what looked like a sun for a head. A sun god? Between the sun god and the people was a heavy, curved line that may have represented a shield of protection. A large arrow pointed to a second scene, which looked like a cave with a campfire, tools, water pitchers, and cooking bowls.

Olivia and Alex, with the help of others, worked their way down to the ledge.

"Look at this, Olivia," said an excited Jenny.

Olivia studied both pictographs. "Wow, I'll bet these are really old! The Tukadeka probably made these paintings." Then her eyes followed a second arrow, revealing an opening in the rock wall, just large enough for an adult human to access. She peered into the opening.

"Jenny—come here and give me a boost!"

Olivia let her eyes adjust from the bright sunlight to the relative darkness of a large cave.

"We've discovered a cave dwelling!"

June 25th (night)

Dear Diary,

I really shouldn't go off by myself anymore. Almost got myself killed! Thanks to Jenny and Olivia and those walkie-talkies, I'm here to tell the tale. What started out as a cry for help turned into a minor miracle. We discovered some ancient cave dwellings! My mom asked Marvin if he could assemble a group to document the pictographs and cave dwellings with photos and GPS readings.

Maybe we'll be in the papers when we get back to civilization! I can see the headlines in the newspapers now: Sara Finds Cave Treasures! Well, maybe more realistically: President's Rafting Party Discovers Sheepeaters' Cave. Either way, that's pretty awesome!

Sara

Chapter 14

The Soak

The river party spent the night at Sheep Creek Camp to explore the Tukadeka Cavern, as Olivia had named it. They found what amounted to a small village inside with rooms and ladders that reached up to three levels in some places. Some rooms were small—probably bedrooms—and others appeared to be designed for larger gatherings. All in all, it looked like the cavern may have housed over two hundred people. A small group explored the cavern, taking as many photographs as possible but trying to leave everything just the way they'd found it. When they got back to civilization, they would report their findings. Experts in history, archeology, and social sciences would most likely comb every inch and write detailed papers to publish in scientific journals. This was, indeed, an extremely rare find.

While the cave-dwelling group was away documenting and exploring, some took advantage of the pause on the river to hike, read books by the river, or visit the nearby hot springs. Olivia and Jenny decided to take President Langford and Sara over to one of the hot pools. Alex and a few of the crew joined them.

During the half-mile hike to the hot pools, they chatted about the day's events. At one point, Olivia spotted a very large bird hammering away at a ponderosa pine.

"That's a pileated woodpecker!" Olivia pointed out.

The bird was making a real racket while it searched for insects and was creating a rectangular hole in the tree in the process. Sara had never seen such a beautiful bird. It was about the size of a large crow and had a long neck, a fiery red crest on top of its head, and bold black and white stripes down its sides.

"Definitely camera-worthy!" exclaimed Sara.

After watching him another five minutes and taking some photos, the group continued on their hike through the woods, enjoying the soft silence that only a forest can provide.

Olivia finally broke that silence. "Those are the Sheepeater hot pools up ahead on the right. There are three pools that range from lukewarm to very hot!"

"Mom, what causes these hot pools to show up in the middle of nowhere?" Sara asked.

"They're caused by fissures or openings in the Earth's crust that bring heat up from the center of the Earth."

They arrived at the edge of the pools. They could smell the sulfur coming from them and watch the steam drifting into the air. Since everyone had bathing suits on under their hiking clothes, they started shedding their shorts, sock, and boots.

"Last one in is a rotten egg!" hollered Jenny.

Olivia held back to get a photograph with her camera. "Say 'pileated!'"

Chapter 15

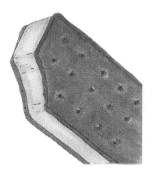

The Haystack

The next morning, the group finally pushed off Sheep Creek. Next stop: the Flying B Ranch, about two miles downriver. The Flying B was one of those iconic river stops that had been supporting rafters for a long time.

"OK. All ashore who's going ashore!" bellowed Marvin. "We'll get some water here and maybe talk to the Bennetts. Most importantly, this is your one and only chance to eat one of their delicious ice cream bars!"

Of course, with visions of frozen treats dancing in their heads, everybody beached their crafts and made a beeline for the line to buy ice cream bars.

While eating their ice cream under the shade of the trees, Olivia and Jenny began to tell Sara about what was next on the river.

"About a half-mile downstream, we are going to hit Haystack and Bernard Creek Rapids. At low water," described Jenny, "they are two distinct rapids. But at high water, like today, they are one big roller coaster ride and definitely hard to figure out. And there is one great big boulder at the end of Bernard that we want to avoid or it's going to be dump truck city!"

Sara's eyebrows knitted as she tried to figure that one out.

"You know," said Olivia, "like a dump truck dumping its load? The raft stays upright but the passengers get unloaded—into the river!"

"Oh. But that will never happen with you guys driving."

"Never say never," Jenny pointed out. "The river does some crazy things at Haystack/Bernard. Isn't that right, Marvin?"

"You bet. I've seen many a raft go into the large rock at Bernard, and it's not pretty when that happens. Bodies flying all over the place!"

"Well, *that's* a comforting thought," mused Sara.

Soon they were back on the water and heard the familiar rumbling of upcoming rapids. "Here comes Haystack. Stay left! Watch that hole on the right!" yelled Jenny.

Olivia guided the raft left of the holes and then calmly rode the surf through Haystack. One down, one to go. But Bernard was dead ahead, and the water was running hard! Olivia was heading directly for that large, sharp rock right in the middle of Bernard!

Sara began to say a prayer.

"On my command . . . hard right, *now!*"

All four put everything they had into it. Just at the last second, the raft pulled right and missed the rock by inches! They spun completely around in a full circle, but by then it didn't matter. They were through Bernard!

"Holy moly, that was close!" yelled Jenny.

"Yeah," responded Olivia, shaking her head. "But that's how you have to do Bernard at high water! Beats dump trucking!"

The rest of the day was pretty normal—they faced mostly class II rapids that were more fun than challenging. At one point, they saw two otters playing nearby, diving and then bobbing their heads above water as if challenging the rafters to jump in the water and play with them.

"Look at those cute guys playing!" exclaimed Sara. "I'm going to call them Susie and Sam! Wow! It looks like Susie is waving at us!"

When they saw the sweep boat pull into Grassy Flat Two Camp, they were all ready to relax around the campfire.

Chapter 16

The Ride

During lunch at Short Creek Camp, Marvin described what they were going to do next. Rusty had been sent ahead to scout the Cold Springs Wave Train. If the conditions were just right, Sara would get to experience something special.

"I know what this is all about!" Olivia said with a nod and a wink.

"Oh yeah!" Jenny chimed in. "Get out your spurs and chaps! It's time to go bull ridin'!"

Sure enough, Rusty came back with good news. "It's perfect today, Marvin. A nice, big, long wave train—running at a class II+. And the big pool at the end can catch anyone that gets bucked off."

Marvin spent the next few minutes describing to the president what happens with bull riding. "So, we'll put

Sara right at the front of the raft. She'll hold onto the rope and have her feet over the edge. You'll be sitting right behind Sara so that you can share in the experience. Olivia will be the oarsman and Jenny and Andrew Vogt, one of our rescue swimmers, will be in the boat as well. We've done this many times and everyone always has a great time. Sound OK?"

President Langford responded, "Sounds like a blast. Sara?"

"Sure, Mom! Let's do it!

When everyone had eaten and cleaned up, they shoved off for Cold Springs Creek. About a quarter-mile from the wave train, Jenny helped Sara get positioned at the front of the boat. Again, the rumble told everyone they were getting close to the rapids.

Olivia went through her checks. "Ready ma'am?"

"Ready!"

"Ready, Sara?"

Sara tucked her left hand into the rope. "Ready!"

"Then . . . ride 'em, cowgirl!"

Up and down went Sara, riding the highs and the lows and getting soaked in the process. Her right hand was flying around, keeping her balance. "Get along little doggie!" she yelled.

The waves had quite an effect on the raft. The front of the boat would start to "taco" and then straighten back out. Finally, the long wave train settled into a riffle, and eventually into the big pool that Rusty had described.

"That's how you ride a bull!" exclaimed Sara. "He was bucking and swaying and was trying to throw me off the whole way. But I hung in there and lasted longer than ten seconds. I didn't even need any of those rodeo clowns!"

Once they hit the pool, Sara clambered back to her normal position and got high fives from her mom, Jenny, and Andrew. The smile on her face would have lit up a small town!

Chapter 17

The Dream

Olivia was having a dream. Or was it more of a nightmare? She was playing for the Bighorn Sheep softball team against their arch rival, the Black Bears. Olivia's coach, Mister Trout, was the worst coach in the world. All he ever cared about was winning. No fundamentals, no teamwork, no fun—just winning. Olivia and Jenny had spent their first ten games on the bench. No grass under their feet, just splinters in their bums. Not one at-bat for either one of them. Nada. Niente.

The Sheep were ahead by one run, but there was a huge storm brewing—one of those big, black-cloud things that was coming on fast. They were in the fifth inning. If the storm hit before the inning was over, they would have to start over with a new game. Coach Trout was willing to do anything to get the inning over with. Five innings would make it a complete game and he would win the game! The Bighorn Sheep needed to make two more outs—and *fast*. Coach Trout knew just what to do.

"Olivia! Jenny! Grab a bat! Get up there and strike out on three pitches!"

"C'mon, Jenny," Olivia whispered to her teammate. "Let's go get a hit!"

The Black Bear pitcher was tough—she looked like a bear that hadn't eaten all winter and was licking her chops for something good to eat: a batter! She had a wicked fastball, an unbelievable sinker, and an off-speed pitch that literally floated to the plate. A batter had time to swing twice before that floater got to the plate. Olivia dug in and readied herself for the first pitch. In came the fastball at seventy miles per hour. Olivia swung with all her might.

"Strike one!" yelled the umpire.

"She's coming with the sinker next!" yelled Jenny.

Wrong. In came the floater. Olivia practically wrapped herself into a pretzel trying to hit it. "Strike two!" yelled the ump.

Just then . . . Olivia awoke to the sound of footsteps outside her tent. She checked her watch. It was 5:30 AM. The crew members would be getting up shortly to start cooking breakfast. Jenny and Sara were still sleeping.

She peeked outside the front of their tent.

"What the . . ." she whispered to herself. Silently creeping past her tent were two men she had never seen before.

Chapter 18

The Interlopers

O livia silently reached for her walkie-talkie. Barely whispering, she called Agent Alex.

"Ironman, this is Penny One. Come in Ironman, over."

"This is Ironman, over."

"Don't look now, Alex, but we've got some strange men in camp. Two men just walked by our tent. Over."

"Is Sara with you? Over."

"She's fine. She's still sleeping. We're all OK. Over"

"OK. Wake her up, keep her calm, and stay in the tent until I call you. We'll take care of this. Out."

Alex's tentmate, Jon, woke up at the sound of the walkie-talkie. Both agents reached for their weapons and crept out onto the grass. They quickly moved toward the president's tent.

Alex dispensed with the normal "tent knock." He unzipped the tent's front fly and stuck his head in. "Ma'am. You OK?"

The president's bodyguard, Marsha, was quickly awake.

"Ah . . . yeah, Alex. We're OK. What's going on?"

"Got somebody in camp who doesn't belong here. Draw your weapon and be at the ready. Stay in the tent. Jon and I are going to find out what's going on."

Alex and Jon began their search of the camp. It didn't take long before they saw two men sneaking around through the shadows. With hand signals, Alex and Jon snuck up behind the interlopers.

"Hold it right there, you two. Don't move! Hands in the air!" Alex commanded.

"Don't shoot! We're just photographers!" one of them pleaded.

Sure enough, as two sets of hands went into the air, the agents saw that each stranger was carrying a camera.

"Jon, take the cameras from them and handcuff them. Now, lie flat on the ground and tell us what you are up to!"

"We could make a lot of money if we could get photos of the president and her party going down the river! The supermarket rags pay big bucks for these kinds of shots!" the tall one explained.

"None of these photos are going to see the light of day!" exclaimed Jon. "And your cameras have now been confiscated by the federal government. It's time to read you your rights!"

By now, most of the campers had come out of tents and were wondering what was going on. It turned out that the photographers had spent the last few days in Salmon, trying to find out where the president's rafting party might be on the river. They then had paid someone to fly them into the Flying B airport and had hiked along the river by moonlight all night to reach the Grassy Flat Two Camp. They were going to set up behind some rocks and take photos while everyone was having breakfast and as they pushed off down the river. Instead, they were escorted into a raft by the trailing security team and taken by helicopter to Boise to be booked properly.

"So much for all that money they were going to make," observed Jenny.

June 27th (Morning)

Dear Diary,

Just when you think you've seen it all! This morning I woke up to find that there were two strange men snooping around our campsite and trying to take photos of us! Alex and Agent Jon arrested them! Paparazzi! Maybe they'll spend a few days cooling their heels in the slammer and will think twice about doing something that stupid again!

My mom is used to this kind of thing and all, so she doesn't get too upset about it. She knows the Secret Service will do their jobs and keep us safe.

Oh well . . . just another morning on the river! :-)

Sara

Chapter 19

The Cave

After breakfast the next morning, Marvin gathered everyone together.

"We are going to do some kayaking today. But first we're going to play tourist. About a mile downriver, we'll stop and check out some pictographs in Rattlesnake Cave. As some of you know, pictographs are paintings on rock. In this case, they were probably painted by the Shoshone Tukadeka, otherwise known as the Sheepeater Indians."

"Why do they call it Rattlesnake Cave?" asked Sara with trepidation. "I really hate snakes! Are there any rattlesnakes in that cave?"

"It's more of an overhang and a shallow cave. The pictographs are on both sedimentary rock and on a granite wall. But don't worry," he laughed, "I've been into that place more than a dozen times and have never seen a rattlesnake!"

"I thought I saw one once on our trip last year," whispered Olivia to Jenny. "But I just caught some movement out of the corner of my eye—and then it was gone."

"I've never seen any snakes there." Jenny responded. "But about four years ago I was on a raft trip with my parents. We walked up to Rattlesnake Cave and saw that the Infamous Stringdusters were actually playing some of their music there. Now, *that* was kind of cool."

A half hour later, the president's group was hiking up the trail to the cave.

"Look at this, Sara," the president directed, pointing to the figures at the overhang. "What do you think this is?"

"Maybe a bird? I think these are feathers hanging down from wings. Wow. Olivia says these paintings could be thousands of years old."

"C'mon, Sara, let's check out the cave!" Jenny said enthusiastically.

Following Olivia and Jenny, Sara stepped into the shallow cave. She immediately noticed the dark sedimentary rock on the wall of the cave. Painted in red on pink granite were a number of human figures and what looked like sheep or deer.

Sara was amazed. "I can just imagine Native Americans

creating this cave art! I wonder if it was done by men or women? Maybe both."

Just then, from the back part of the cave came an eerie sound. *"Thrrrrrrrrrrrrrrrrrrrrrrrrr."*

As one, the girls swiveled around in the direction of the noise. There, barely discernible in the shadows, was the outline of a coiled rattler, about fifteen feet away! Its glowing, beady eyes were fixed on them.

"Back up slowly, Sara," said Olivia in measured tones. "Slowly and quietly. No sudden movements. That's it . . . good. We don't need any snake bites on this trip."

Once they were out of the cave, they let out a collective breath of relief.

Sara moved toward her mom. "Oh my God, Mom. There was a rattlesnake in there. Let's get back to the water!"

"My bad, ma'am," said Marvin. "We should have checked out that cave ahead of time for you."

"No harm done, Marvin. You guys are doing a great job. And as Ranger Sheldon said, we're in wild animal territory and we should expect these kinds of things. Let's get back to the river and enjoy the rest of our journey."

June 27th (Day)

Dear Diary,

A rattlesnake! I have never been so scared! OMG! My heart was practically beating out of my chest! Once we got out of that cave and over to the rest of the group, I was finally able to breathe again! And I felt even better when we got back in the rafts. No more snakes for me! Yuck!

Sara

Chapter 20

The Kayaking

*J*ust after mile seventy-seven, the rafting party reached the Impassable Canyon. This was where Big Creek met the Middle Fork and where the massive granite walls became so steep that trail builders had to stop building a hiking trail along the river.

"Sara, look back at the waterfall over there," said Olivia, pointing. "That is Waterfall Creek Falls. You ought to see it in May. It is just . . . unbelievable! Water just rages off those boulders! When we get back to camp tonight, remind me to show you the photos I took last month."

For their lunch stop, they pulled into Elk Bar Camp, one of the prettiest spots on the river. Marvin gathered Sara, Olivia, Jenny, and President Langford together after they had finished their sandwiches, peanut butter, celery, and fruit. These four had volunteered together and would have a chance to ride the kayaks over the next section.

Ron Hall, an expert kayaker who had been one of those trailing the party on the trip, spoke up. "We're going into a short but fun stretch of water with some riffles and a really cool class II rapids. Olivia and Jenny, of course, have done this before. Madame President,

you and Sara have had a few turns on the kayaks already, but in calmer water. So . . . this will be a little more of a challenge. We've got your inflatable kayaks at the ready. We're going over the Crystal Pool riffle first followed by the Veil Cave Rapids. I want you to pay attention and follow me as we go over both. And, most important of all, enjoy the experience!"

As per usual, Marvin's sweep boat led the way. Next was Rusty Deibert driving Sara's raft with one of the rescue swimmers, Andrew Vogt. Ron was the lead kayaker, followed by Jenny, the president, Sara, and Olivia. They all followed the left-hand bend in the river, moving left with the current. As they entered the Crystal Pool riffle, they almost brushed against a vertical wall of granite that reached up hundreds of feet.

Sara exclaimed, "I can almost touch the wall! And the water is so clear here. Look at the rocks underneath our kayaks!"

Next up was Veil Cave Rapids. This was a continuous wave, a little like the riffle, only with much higher waves. It felt to Sara as if her kayak was almost floating above the water. She followed her mom into the rumbling current. Up and down, up and down she went. *This is a blast!* she thought.

Just when she thought she had mastered the art of kayaking, her craft spun a little sideways. In a bit of a panic, Sara pulled with the wrong oar and over she went, into the forty-degree water!

"Sara's down!" yelled Olivia.

Chapter 21

The Rescue

"Think, Sara!" she chided herself. "I'm alive, I can breathe—but I need to get out from under this boat!" She pushed up on the side of the kayak but, just then, the wave action caused the craft to go too high, and she lost her leverage. "*I've got to push hard when the kayak is lowest and just starting to go back up,*" she thought.

At the sound of Olivia's cry, Andrew had jumped into the water and was breast-stroking against the current with his head above the waves, looking for Sara. All he saw was her kayak about forty yards upriver.

Sara figured she had one more chance to get this thing off of her. As the kayak came down from the next wave, she waited and then pushed with all her might.

The kayak slipped away and she was free! She got her feet facing downriver and yelled, "Help!"

By now, Andrew could see her and started swimming freestyle to get over to her. She was moving quickly with the current. Could he reach her? With three powerful strokes, he was able to reach out and grab her floatation device.

"I've got you, Sara. Relax. We'll be in the sweep boat in a few minutes." They rode the waves through the rest of the rapid and entered the Veil Cave grotto. Sara looked up to see a fine-mist waterfall flowing over the face of a deep cave.

Marvin extended an oar from his boat. Sara grabbed it and was hoisted into the boat with an assist from Andrew. And that was that. Before you could say Veil Cave Rapids, it was over and all was right with the world.

June 27th (Night)

Dear Diary,

 Well, here we are relaxing at Ship Island Camp. I no longer get Aaron and Andrew mixed up, lol. Andrew Vogt is my new hero! It was such a relief when he grabbed me in the water today and brought me over to the sweep boat. We pulled over to the shore, where Mom helped me get out of my wet clothes and into some dry ones. After drying my hair with a towel, I was ready to move on.

The kayaking was awesome—well, until I went into the water. Thanks to everyone—especially you, Andrew the Great!

Sara

Chapter 22

The Stories

*J*enny, turning to Sara, whispered, "You never know if these stories are true or made up, but they sure are fun to hear!"

Marvin, as the leader of the river party, threw another log on the fire, settled into his chair, and led off with the first campfire story of the night.

"You should have been with us on one of our trips down the river in 2003. It was so awesome! This is a story about how Cramer Creek Rapids got a whole lot bigger and badder in just one day. We have to go over Cramer Creek tomorrow, so pay attention. It's gonna be our longest and toughest rapid of the whole trip—and I'm not kidding! Anyway, in July of that year, there was a bad fire where Cramer Creek meets the Middle Fork.

It took out a lot of trees. When they opened the river back up, we were one of the first groups to ride it. We were camping at Cradle Creek Camp, about five miles downstream from where we are right now. That night, a tremendous thunderstorm came roaring in and caused a flash flood down Cramer Creek and into the Middle Fork.

"We didn't know what we had gotten ourselves into. Let me tell you, I've never seen anything like it. When we got to Cramer Creek, new, gigantic boulders were all over the place, and the water was a raging torrent! We did our best to scout it, but we still spilled three boats, including the sweep boat, which I had never seen happen before! The good news is that Cache Bar, our take-out spot, was only another half-mile downriver. We basically limped into that place like a bunch of wet rag dolls—and that's the truth! Ain't that right, Rusty?"

"Yeah, Marvin, you got it right. Darndest thing I ever saw in twenty-five years on the river!"

Most were impressed with Marvin's story, especially knowing that he didn't usually exaggerate.

"Who else wants to tell a story?" asked Marvin.

"I'll take a crack at it!" yelled Merlin, another of the Deibert Brothers. "This was about ten years ago. We were just cruisin' down the river approaching the Loon Islands. We took a hard right around the bend there, and right smack in the middle of the river was the biggest black bear you ever saw. He got up on his hind legs to greet us and had a big, fat Chinook Salmon in his mouth. Well, we were heading right towards him, and it looked like we were gonna take him out. We all

started yelling "Hey bear!" and swinging our paddles and such, when he decided to yell back! *Roooaaarrrr!* And that's when the fish slipped out of his jaws! He dodged to our left, we turned abruptly right, and that's when his fish......fell right into our boat! It was probably the biggest salmon we had ever seen! Back in those days, they didn't make us throw the fish back in the river, and we figured the fish was dead anyway after having been gutted by two-inch bear teeth! So we cleaned that salmon and had enough fish for all ten of us in our party! Best fish I've ever tasted!"

Everyone started looking around at each other until Olivia spoke up. "Whew," she said, "now *that* was a tall tale!"

Chapter 23

The Favorite Part

Olivia awoke to the sound of raindrops on the tent. *Darn,* she thought, *this is our last day and it has to rain?* She looked at her watch—almost six AM. Time to get up and get going. They were getting an early start so that they could make the last sixteen miles from Ship Island Camp to Cache Bar.

By the time the girls got in line for breakfast, the rain was already letting up. Luckily, it turned out to be just a passing shower.

"We don't need any complications like rain on our last day," Olivia remarked to Sara. "The river has a lot of fun things in store for us today, but it also has some big-time challenges. Rubber, Devil's Tooth, House of Rocks, and Cramer Creek are all class IV rapids. Throw in four other class III rapids, and there is some significant big water on the last ten miles!"

"Yeah, for sure!" proclaimed Jenny. "I like to call this helmet day—as in, we're all going to need our helmets!"

They pushed off at around 7:45 and cruised through Nugget Creek and Cliffside Rapids. It was a good time to talk before the big water.

"So . . . Sara," began Jenny as she manipulated the oars from the rear of the raft. "What do you think of the Middle Fork—like, the whole river experience?"

"It's been one great big adventure from beginning to end!"

"What was your favorite part?" asked Olivia.

"Um . . . probably the Tappan Rapids. Or the talks around the campfire. Maybe . . . finding the cave dwellings! *That* was pretty cool. Or seeing the pileated woodpecker."

Olivia and Jenny began looking at each other with knowing smiles.

"Well," said Sara, seeing the looks on the other girls' faces, "there were *lots* of great parts, so it's hard to say one is better than the other! But I can tell you what the *worst* part was! That ugly, slimy rattlesnake!"

With that, they cruised into Otter Bar Camp for lunch.

Chapter 24

The Big Water

O livia took over for the last nine miles. You could feel the anxiety in the air as they heard the now-familiar rumble of rapids up ahead. Rubber Rapids, the longest ride on the river, and one of the scariest, was coming up fast. Ron would lead everyone in his kayak so that he could circle back in and take photos of everyone running Rubber. First, they would go through the relatively calm Son of Rubber, a class II, before immediately running Son's "big daddy."

Jenny began going through the approach to Rubber with Olivia, yelling as loud as she could. "Remember, there are some huge waves, Olivia—and one of them comes at us from the left bank! We need to turn toward that wave to keep us from flipping!"

"Got it!" Olivia yelled back. And then the rapids became a roar.

Into Rubber Rapids they went. The raft was shoved down hard and it immediately came out of the water. Sara was looking at blue sky. Then down again, and sideways. By now, everyone knew to lean to the high side to stay afloat.

"Wave to left!" Jenny screamed. In unison, Olivia and Jenny forced the raft left, directly into the largest wave they had encountered on the trip. Up went the raft as they met the monster wave head-on. They started to backslide and tilt right.

"High side left!" yelled Olivia. Back down they came, sliding with the wave, only to be righted by a rock just under the surface. With the raft heading directly downstream again, they began the long roller coaster ride to the end of Rubber and a beautiful, long pool.

"Everybody doing OK?" asked Olivia.

"That was a good one!" said Alex enthusiastically. "For a second there, I thought that big wave was going to flip us backward!"

"Unreal!" exclaimed Sara. "Just unreal. That wall of water seemed almost as big as some of those hills in Virginia! If Ron got a good shot of that, I'm going to blow it up and hang it on a White House wall! Hey Mom! Was that super cool or what?"

Chapter 25

The Rocks

"*H*igher water sometimes has its advantages!" cried Jenny.

They all agreed. And, after they caught their breath, they had a fairly easy time with the long, rollicking Hancock Rapids. That was followed by Devil's Tooth, which they cruised through on the left side. But now the group prepared for another wild ride as hundreds of even larger rocks, requiring significant expertise to avoid them, lay ahead for the next five miles.

Olivia had just a few minutes to describe their strategy. "House of Rocks is next, guys. Look for a tree hanging over the rapids. We're going to execute a hard left at that tree to avoid the rocks and the holes. Jenny and Sara will pull. Alex, you'll push. Any questions?"

"OK . . . here it comes . . . now!"

Olivia guided them into the slot with professional perfection. Sara thought, *Oh my God! Look at the size of these boulders!*

They avoided a couple of big keeper holes, and then Olivia brought the raft back around to the center to run the rest of the rapid.

Five minutes later, they were cruising by a rock that jutted up from the river like the Matterhorn itself.

"That's Clamshell Rock!" Jenny pointed out. "Let's take a photo, Olivia!"

Olivia worked the raft over to an eddy by the rock so that everyone could get a good look. Sara had her camera at the ready.

"OK . . . smile, Jenny!"

Chapter 26

The Finish

Cramer Creek was the last big water rapid that they had to negotiate. And, it was a big one! As Marvin had said many times, Cramer Creek could be the toughest on the river.

Olivia, while guiding them through the remaining class II and class III rapids, began to remind them about Cramer Creek. "Cramer Creek used to be a nice cruise into our take-out at Cache Bar. You remember Marvin's story around the campfire last night? He wasn't kidding! Since that big fire of 2003 and the flash flood, it is now one of the most dangerous rapids on the Middle Fork. It has flipped a lot of boats since then. The higher water may help us today—we'll see. When we get there, I will guide the raft through the left-center channel. I want everyone to paddle like mad when I give the signal. Then, when we hit that first big wave, lean into it or it will tip us over backward. Everybody got it?"

And with that, the Middle Fork made a left-hand turn and joined up with the Main Salmon, The River of No Return.

"Woohoo!" yelled Jenny. "We made it to the confluence! Only two and a half miles to go!"

Two miles ahead: the rumbling, ravaging waters of Cramer Creek.

Everyone got quiet as they approached the rapids. Then Olivia screamed, "It's porpoise time! On three, everybody! Row . . . *hard!*"

Into the cauldron of water they went, fast and furious. Down, down, the boat's nose starting to submerge—and then up, up, up. The raft was almost vertical!

"Lean forward!" screamed Jenny.

Sara thought they were going to go flying through the air. "Please. Please. Please." she whispered to herself. "Please let us get through this!"

Back down they came, everyone still on board.

"Keep rowing!" yelled Olivia.

And up, up again. This time, the boat leaned right slightly, causing water to drench them as they landed. *Wooosh!*

"Yeehaw!" yelled Alex again.

Then, with each successive wave, the ups and downs

became less marked, and eventually they smoothed out into a cruise.

Sara looked around, realized that they had survived, and yelled, "We did it! The Paddlers are masters of the river!"

Chapter 27

The Lucky Penny

Up ahead at Cache Bar, it was getting a little crazy. The president's forward team—the communicators and the extra security—had arrived at the take-out. Waiting for them were a few press reporters and photographers from Boise and Missoula.

When the president's sweep boat arrived, a small pep band from Salmon greeted her with a rendition of "Hail to the Chief." The press converged on the president and began to pepper her with questions.

"How was your raft trip, Madame President?"

"Best vacation ever! At times it was challenging. At times it was soooooo relaxing. But it was always fun. And I would just like to say that this river wilderness, this incredible Middle Fork, is an area of unmatched beauty. We need to do everything we can to preserve areas like this so that all Americans can enjoy such spectacular beauty. And, as Ranger Sheldon said at the beginning of our trip, 'It is up to all of us to leave the river in the condition we found it for those that follow us.'"

"Were you ever frightened by the rapids?"

"At times it got a little scary, but we always felt like we were in good hands with our expert river guides!"

Everyone clapped as the president recognized the Deiberts.

"And how about you, Sara, how did you like the river?"

"Oh my God, it was awesome! Every day brought something better and more fun than the last. But there were some dangerous moments. I owe my life to these two girls, Olivia and Jenny, the Lucky Penny Detectives."

Sara pointed to the girls and asked them to step forward. "These girls were unbelievable. They are expert rowers and guides, and they rescued me from a ledge on a cliff. And from a rattlesnake!" she added with a smile.

"Olivia!" yelled one of the reporters. "What makes you girls so successful in riding the river?"

Olivia thought for a second. "I guess it's not *that* difficult if you have some river experience, riders who listen to you, and"—Olivia pulled her lucky penny out of her pocket—"and a lucky penny!"

And that's how the River of No Return trip ended: everyone safe and sound and homeward bound—with extra special thanks to an eagle and a lucky penny.

The End

Chapter 28

The Postscript

July 3rd

Dear Diary,

Tomorrow is the fourth of July. Mom and I are in Massachusetts for the long weekend and will celebrate the birth of our nation by sailing on the USS Constitution. According to the brochure they gave us, she is a three-masted frigate and "the oldest commissioned naval vessel still afloat." Every year, the officers and crew of the Constitution salute the nation with a turnaround cruise in Boston Harbor. This year will be the ship's 225th year of dedicated service to the United States Navy. Wow! I am totally stoked!

But . . . I've got to say that my mind continues to wander back to the Idaho wilderness and the best vacation I've ever had. And the river! I just finished a poem I wrote about the river experience and wanted to share it with you, Diary.

The river flows past granite walls,
Past sandy banks and over falls,
Through quiet air and wind a'blowing,
Always ever, ever flowing.

From rippling stream to ocean sea.
It flows along for you and me.
It swirls about and fairly dances.
We climb aboard and take our chances.

Sara

P.s. To Olivia and Jenny: you guys rock!

Glossary of River Terms

Big water: Fast water, big waves, potential for extreme violence.

Bump: A rock just under the surface of the water that can push a rubber raft up a little.

Channel: A raftable route through a section of river.

Confluence: Where two rivers come together.

Dump truck: When a raft dumps some or all of its passengers but remains upright.

Hole: A place where the basic current is disrupted, usually caused by rocks.

High siding: If a raft is pushed by a wave or caught in a hydraulic, it will often quickly go sideways. In order to stop the raft from flipping on its inside edge, the rafters can climb to the side of the raft furthest downstream, which will also be the side that is highest in the air—hence the name.

Keeper hole: The kind of hole that is difficult to get out of.

Maytagging: Getting caught in a swirling circle of water that won't allow the raft to break out and go downstream. The term is in reference to a Maytag washing machine.

Riffle: A series of small, shallow waves usually over a sand or gravel bottom.

Taco: When the nose or stern of the raft is pulled down under water and buckles to touch the middle.

Take-out: The place on the river where the rafters finish their journey and get back on dry land.

The River Campfire Song

Music: Tom Robin Harris
Text: Craig Vroom

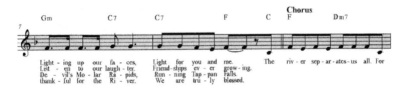

Acknowledgments

This is primarily a fictional story with some historical elements. The idea of a presidential vacation came from a family trip we made in 1994 down the Middle Fork. The Guth Brothers Outfitters were our excellent guides for that trip. They told us the story of when they guided President Jimmy Carter and his family down the Middle Fork, while he was president, in 1978. The adventures that Sara and her mom experience in this story are the product of my imagination and are totally fictional.

The primary resource that helped guide me through all the rapids was Matt Leidecker's wonderfully detailed and accurate book: *The Middle Fork of the Salmon River: A Comprehensive Guide – 4th Edition*

I am indebted to the following friends, family, and Middle Fork experts for reviewing *The River of No Return, Another Lucky Penny Detective Adventure*: Dave Robey, Marnie Sell, Diane Berne, Paul Schild, and my wife, Becky. And a big tip of the hat to Victoria Sell, who told me all about bull riding on the river.

To Jenn Chic, my wonderful illustrator: you have brought my text alive with your fun and fanciful artwork!

Many thanks to Tru Publishing and Fred Johnson for doing such a great job with the cover design, packaging, and editing of *The River of No Return*.

Finally, a big thanks to Tom Robin Harris for composing the music for the song, *"The River Campfire."*

About the Author

Craig Vroom

Award-winning author Craig Vroom, featured in this winter's *Visit McCall Magazine*, writes adventure stories for children. His books include *The Secretous Sign*, *The Riddle of Shipwreck Sound*, *The Tall Trees*, and *Discovering Sharlie: Case of the Missing Sea Serpent*, which won first place in 2015 at Idaho's Top Author Awards (Children's Book Category). Craig has been called the "Dr. Seuss of Idaho" for his amazing ability to tell a story through poetry.

Craig has been invited to present and sign his books at many venues, including the Author Fest of the Rockies, the Baseball Hall of Fame in Cooperstown, New York, and the Festival of Trees in McCall. Craig enjoys visiting classrooms at all grade levels, showing children how reading and writing poetry can be a fun and enriching experience.

Craig's poems capture the adventure that is possible in the imagination of every child. As a lover of the Idaho outdoors, he also strives to combine a spirit of mystique and adventure with wonderful experiences in the natural world.

The River of No Return is Craig's first chapter book.

About the Illustrator

Jenn Chic

Jenn Chic has always loved drawing and considers it a joy and a privilege to work with authors to tell their stories. Especially if pancakes and otters are involved! She studied fine art in university which then led to a career as a chef before becoming a mom.

Jenn has been on her own rafting adventures in Canada, Thailand, and Japan. Although not much for "bull riding the rapids," she does love watching all the wildlife from the river and roasting marshmallows around the campfire.

She lives in the mountains of Canada with her husband and her two greatest inspirations, her son and her daughter. She is grateful to her sister who lives in Idaho and who introduced her to Craig and got this collaboration started. It's been such fun!

69333137R00071

Made in the USA
Columbia, SC
21 August 2019